Gho
Elementary®

Red, White, and BOO!

Find out more spooky secrets about

Ghostville Elementary®

#1 *Ghost Class*
#2 *Ghost Game*
#3 *New Ghoul in School*
#4 *Happy Haunting!*
#5 *Stage Fright*
#6 *Happy Boo-Day to You!*
#7 *Hide-and-Spook*
#8 *Ghosts Be Gone!*
#9 *Beware of the Blabbermouth!*
#10 *Class Trip to the Haunted House*
#11 *The Treasure Haunt*
#12 *Frights! Camera! Action!*
#13 *Guys and Ghouls*
#14 *Frighting Like Cats and Dogs*
#15 *A Very Haunted Holiday*
#16 *Red, White, and BOO!*
#17 *No Haunting Zone*

Ghostville Elementary®

Red, White, and BOO!

by Marcia Thornton Jones
and
Debbie Dadey

illustrated by Guy Francis

A
LITTLE **APPLE**
PAPERBACK

SCHOLASTIC INC.
New York Toronto London Auckland Sydney
Mexico City New Delhi Hong Kong Buenos Aires

To Shannon Penney—
a Red, White, and BOO editor!
—MTJ and DD

ISBN-13: 978-0-439-88364-1
ISBN-10: 0-439-88364-4

12 11 10 9 8 7 6 5 4 3 2 7 8 9 10 11 12/0

Printed in the U.S.A. 40
First printing, February 2007

Contents

THE LEGEND

Sleepy Hollow Elementary School's
Online Newspaper

This Just In: Banners! Buttons! Posters!

The third graders at Sleepy Hollow Elementary are celebrating Presidents' Day with an election of their own. I'm not sure who will win, but one thing is sure: Whoever becomes classroom president must be ready to deal with a spooky citizen or two. That's because there's bound to be trouble when the ghosts start casting votes of their own!

Stay tuned for more as the election news rolls in!

Yours truly,
Justin Thyme

1
Democracy in Action

"I have a wonderful idea," Mr. Morton said.

Andrew groaned. So did the other kids in the classroom. They had been in Mr. Morton's third-grade class long enough to know that when Mr. Morton had a "wonderful" idea it meant work, work, and more work. The third graders sat up in their desks to listen, even though they figured it would be bad news. They weren't the only ones who wanted to hear.

Above Mr. Morton's head, the air thickened. It swirled. It sparkled until . . .

POP . . .

POP!

Two ghosts appeared.

To most people, the stories about ghosts living in the basement of Sleepy

Hollow Elementary School were just that: stories. But to Nina, Cassidy, and Jeff, the ghosts were real. Very real. That's because the ghosts allowed only these three friends to see and hear them.

"I hope this means lots of work," the ghost boy named Ozzy said with a laugh. Ozzy was a pesky kind of ghost. He liked seeing Cassidy, Nina, and Jeff work.

Becky, his ghost sister giggled. "If they're busy, then they can't bother *us*!" Becky loved to dance. She didn't like to be disturbed while she twirled through the air.

A third ghost stuck his head out of a picture hanging on the wall. Edgar had his journal and a stubby pencil in his hand. He liked writing stories.

Nina wished the ghosts would be quiet so she could hear the teacher's announcement better. Every time the ghosts appeared, goose bumps raced down her suntanned arms and she shivered. The

ghosts had never hurt anyone, but she still thought they were scary.

Just then, Mr. Morton cleared his throat. “Democracy!” he shouted, startling the ghosts.

Ozzy jumped, and his head disappeared into the ceiling. Ozzy’s feet dangled back and forth as he tried to wiggle free. He finally pulled his body and head out with a loud sucking sound. Becky did a somersault through the air. She landed upside down in the bucket the kids used to wash

the chalkboard. Becky's hair dripped chalky water when she popped back out. Nina started to giggle, but covered her mouth when Becky gave her such a cold glare that it turned the soggy ghost's hair into icicles. Edgar disappeared back into his picture.

"Democracy," Mr. Morton said again. "It's what makes our country so grand."

The kids already knew that because they had been studying democracy for President's Day. They knew about elections, campaigning, and voting.

Mr. Morton smiled like he was telling them about an Easter Bunny surprise. "To celebrate our history of great leaders," he said, "we're going to hold our own election for a class president! We'll see democracy in action!"

"Me! Me! Me!" someone shouted. "Vote for ME!"

Cassidy, Jeff, and Nina looked into the air over their teacher's head.

"Oh, no," Nina whimpered.

2
Ghost of a Chance

"I want to be president!" Ozzy shouted.

At her brother's words, Becky went into a tizzy. She spun around Ozzy so quickly that she got dizzy. Her long skirt tangled around her legs, and her hair whipped three A++ papers off the bulletin board. Nina got dizzy, too. When Becky's body finished spinning, her head kept going. "I think I should be president," she said, grabbing her head to stop it from twirling.

Ozzy squished his sister's head down into her shoulders. "Don't be silly. Girls can't be president. Besides, I'm bigger than you, so I should be president," he said.

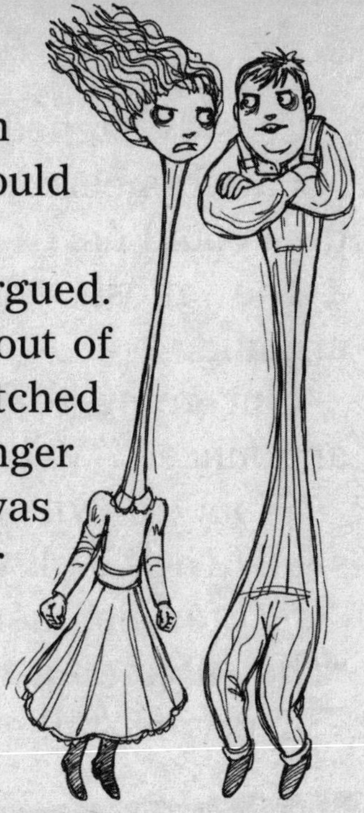

"Oh, yeah?" Becky argued. She popped her head out of her shoulders and stretched her neck. It grew longer and longer until she was twice as tall as her brother.

Ozzy wasn't about to be outdone by his little sister. He twisted his body like taffy until he was even taller than Becky. Before long, Becky and Ozzy's heads were both squashed against the ceiling.

Cassidy heard a tap-tap-tapping from the picture frame near Jeff's desk. It was Edgar. He was pounding a sign on the tree inside his picture where he liked to hide. In neat block letters it read, "EDGAR FOR PRESIDENT!"

Cassidy sighed. Jeff shook his head. Nina whimpered, but there was nothing they could do.

The ghosts weren't the only ones arguing.

"I'm going to be president," Andrew announced. "Vote for me."

"Nobody will vote for you," Carla said. "They'll all vote . . ."

". . . for me," her twin sister Darla said. "They'll vote for me."

Everyone talked at once. Mr. Morton

clapped his hands to get their attention. "Before anyone runs for president," he explained, "you will have to decide on your platform."

Andrew stood up. "I'll use my desk as a stage," he said.

"No, no, no," Mr. Morton said. "In a campaign, the platform is what you stand *for*, not what you stand *on*. So right now, everyone take out a piece of paper and make a list of things you would do if you were class president."

The kids worked on their platforms until it was time for recess. When most of the class had filed out the playground door, Nina pulled Cassidy and Jeff aside. "We have to make the ghosts understand that this election isn't for them or they might be disappointed," she whispered. "Nobody likes a disappointed ghost."

"Ghosts can't run for class president," Jeff announced to Ozzy, Becky, Edgar, and any other ghost that might be listening.

Ozzy popped into view and puffed up like a porcupine. He even had quills instead of hair. "Of course I can run for president. I've been a citizen of this classroom far longer than you. I'd be a better president than George Washington or Abraham Lincoln."

"What kind of class president would you make?" Cassidy asked. "You don't even know who the President of the United States is."

Becky got very red in the face — as well as the arms and legs and hands and eyes. "Of course we know who is President! Our teacher made us study it! It's Grover Cleveland . . . and we know everything it takes to be good leaders. Just wait and see!"

With that, Becky and Ozzy popped out of sight.

"I have a very bad feeling about this," Cassidy said.

Jeff nodded. "This election doesn't stand a *ghost* of a chance."

3
Trouble

At recess, Cassidy, Jeff, and Nina perched on the top of the monkey bars with the bright blue sky above them. Even though the February wind was cold, the sun shone warm on their backs. All around them kids played kickball and soccer. Nina wanted to play, too, but she worried about the ghosts. "The ghosts think that Grover Cleveland is still President," she said.

Cassidy's blond curls blew in the breeze. "How can we make them understand that a lot of things have changed in the last hundred years?"

"Just think, one hundred years ago movies probably weren't even invented." Jeff shuddered. He liked movies so much, he couldn't imagine life without them. It

was his dream to make the world's best scary movies one day.

"Were there even cars?" Nina asked.

"There definitely weren't computers," Cassidy said. Her friends knew how much she loved computer games.

"It would stink not to be able to watch cartoons," Jeff said. His friends nodded.

"I don't think I would have liked living back then," Nina said. "It must have been horrible. Just think. No bathrooms! No televisions! No cell phones!"

Cassidy shrugged. "They had to work hard. My grandfather is seventy years old and he calls when he was growing up the good old days."

"Why?" Jeff asked.

"Because they had more time for family, and they weren't always rushing around," Cassidy said.

Nina nodded. "Sometimes I eat dinner in the car between soccer practice and guitar lessons."

"I bet they didn't do that a hundred years ago," Jeff said.

"The ghosts didn't have cars, guitar lessons, or soccer teams. They don't have a clue about what life is like now. Maybe if we teach the ghosts about how things have changed, they'll realize they have a lot to learn before one of them could be class president," Cassidy suggested.

Jeff nodded. "That's a great idea. If they find out how different things are, maybe they'll see they're wrong about the election."

"Surely, they'll understand that a ghost can't be class president," Cassidy said.

"Maybe," Nina said. "But I have a bad feeling that this class election is campaigning for trouble."

4
Timeline

Later in the day, when their class went to the library, Jeff checked out the biggest book. “Why did you choose that huge thing?” Nina asked as Jeff lugged it into the classroom.

Jeff sat the book on his desk. It fell open to a page about cooking. Jeff pointed to a woodstove. “This shows how people cooked a long time ago.”

Cassidy tapped the other page. Her finger rested on the picture of a microwave oven. “This is how we cook at my house most of the time.”

“You checked out a whole book about cooking?” Andrew said when he walked by. “How dumb is that?” Andrew was not the kind of kid who cared about cooking.

All he cared about was eating more cookies than anyone else.

"It's not just about cooking," Jeff explained. "It's about how things have changed in the last one hundred years."

Andrew tossed his magazine onto his desk. "Who cares about how things were a hundred years ago?" he asked.

Mr. Morton followed Carla and Darla into the classroom and overheard Andrew. "I think history is very interesting," Mr. Morton told his students. "By studying the past, we can make better decisions for our future."

"Then you'll love Jeff's book," Andrew mumbled.

Mr. Morton flipped through the pages of Jeff's book. "Look at that," Mr. Morton said. "Aren't you glad we don't have one-room schoolhouses anymore?"

Cassidy giggled when she saw one of the pictures. "Andrew should be happy.

He probably would have spent all his time with the dunce hat on."

"Let's be nice, Cassidy," Mr. Morton warned, although he couldn't help smiling just a bit.

While Mr. Morton looked at the book, the air above him glittered green. Ozzy appeared and floated above the teacher.

"All these changes are amazing," Mr. Morton told Jeff. "As a matter of fact, this book gives me a great idea."

Andrew groaned. Mr. Morton had already had *one* idea today. "This could go along with our class election," Mr. Morton said, rubbing his hands together. He hurried to the board and wrote:

A timeline of our presidents

"What's a timeline?" a girl named Barbara asked.

"That's where you put down things that have happened . . ." Carla explained.

". . . in certain years," her twin sister Darla added.

"Exactly," Mr. Morton said, his eyes sparkling behind his glasses. "Our time-line could tell about the presidents and how things have changed. We could end it with a picture of who wins the class election."

"That would be me!" Andrew said.

"ME!" Ozzy said at exactly the same time.

"ME!" came Edgar's voice from the picture hanging on the wall.

"ME! ME! ME!" screamed Becky.

It was a good thing most of the class couldn't hear the ghosts.

Nina sighed. Everyone wanted to be president. How would they ever solve this election mess?

5
Bubble Gum and Mud Pits

For the rest of the week, the kids worked together. Each group had to research what happened during a certain period of time, including who was President. Mr. Morton hung a long roll of butcher paper on the wall so the groups could start their timeline sketches.

Andrew didn't care about what happened a long time ago. He only cared about what happened NOW. And right now, he was determined to win the election.

"Vote for me," he told a group working on the Civil War era. He handed them a campaign sign with his picture in the middle.

"Why would we vote for you?" Carla asked.

"You're nothing but a bully," added Darla.

"Because," Andrew told them, "if you vote for me, I promise we'll have bubble gum for morning snack."

"Mr. Morton would never allow that," Carla said.

"He'd have to," Andrew told them. "I'd be president."

Carla and Darla turned away from Andrew. Drawn above their sketch of Abraham Lincoln was a faint picture of a ghost wearing overalls and sticking out his tongue. "Hey!" Darla said. "Who drew that on our section?"

"Not me," Andrew said. "I am not a crook."

"Vote for me," he told the group working on the section about World War II.

"I wouldn't vote for you if you were the last candidate on earth," Allison said.

"But if you vote for me, I'll build a mud pit on the playground," Andrew said.

"A mud pit would be awesome!" Alex said.

"We could push the girls in," Danny said.

"Nuh-uh," said Barbara, "because we'd push you in first."

While the group was arguing, Andrew stuck up one of his campaign signs near their mural.

"Hey, who drew that?" Barbara asked

when she looked back at their sketch. A ghostly figure flew on a cloud above Barbara's World War II airplanes.

"Read my lips. I did not do it," Andrew said as he moved down the line. He stopped at Nina's group. She had sketched a picture of Grover Cleveland.

"Nooooooo," Becky the ghost told Nina. "That's not how he REALLY looked." Nina erased Grover Cleveland's mustache and started over, but Becky still wasn't happy. She tried to grab Nina's

pencil, but she wasn't concentrating hard enough. Her ghostly fingers passed right through Nina's hand. Nina jumped at the bone-chilling cold and dropped the pencil to the floor.

Andrew walked up and tapped Nina on the shoulder. "Vote for me," Andrew told Nina, Cassidy, and Jeff.

"Not a chance," Cassidy said. "They're voting for me."

"YOU!" Andrew said with a laugh. "Everyone knows a girl can't be president. Just look at the pictures everyone is drawing. They're all MEN!" All of the kids stopped to look at the drawings. Sure enough, not a single woman was pictured.

"You're right," Cassidy said. "All the Presidents of the United States have been men. That means only one thing. It's time for a change!"

"No, it's not," Jeff said. "But don't worry. Andrew won't be president. I will."

Andrew threw his posters on the floor and poked Jeff in the chest. "Forget it, Jeff. I'm going to win this election."

"Why would we vote for a candidate who looks like THAT?" Nina asked with a giggle. While they had been talking, someone had drawn on Andrew's campaign posters. Boogers oozed out his nose and slime poured from his ears. Nina knew exactly who had done it because she had seen Ozzy's ghostly shape concentrating

to hold a marker. Of course, Andrew had no idea that ghosts were hovering near.

"Whoever did this is in trouble," Andrew said, his fingers curled into fists. "BIG trouble!"

6
Peanut Butter President

The next morning, Andrew was fit to be tied. “Somebody smeared peanut butter all over my campaign buttons,” he complained. He wanted everyone to wear a pin with his picture on it, but nobody would touch them now.

Jeff grinned as he hung his own poster near the door to their classroom. “Looks like someone thinks Andrew is NUTS for trying to be class president.”

Jeff knew exactly who had ruined the pins because he could see Ozzy dipping a ghostly finger inside an empty peanut butter jar.

“We didn’t want one of your buttons anyway,” Carla said.

“We have our own,” added Darla.

A group of girls skipped into the classroom. Some of them wore buttons with Carla's picture. The others had a picture of Darla.

"Why would anyone vote for either of you?" Andrew asked.

"Simple," Darla said. "Our father is an expert baker . . ."

". . . and I promise to bring cookies to everyone that votes for me," finished Carla.

"I'll bring *chocolate-chip* cookies if you vote for me," Darla interrupted.

"Vote for me and I'll give everyone *giant* sugar cookies," Carla said. "With icing!"

As the two sisters argued over which cookies tasted better, Andrew tossed his buttons in the trash can. A cloud of glitter formed nearby. Nina recognized the shape of Huxley, the ghost dog. Huxley nosed around the trash can, trying to find the peanut butter. Nina knew ghosts had to concentrate very hard to move things. All the ghosts, that is, except Huxley. For some reason, he pushed over the trash can in no time at all.

Peanut-butter–covered buttons scattered across the floor.

"Look at what Andrew did!" Carla announced.

"I didn't do it," Andrew argued. "Jeff did!"

"I didn't touch your pins," Jeff said.

"I know what this is," Andrew said.

"Jeff's using dirty and STICKY politics. He ruined my buttons and my posters because he wants to win the election."

"I did not," Jeff said.

"It won't work," Carla said. "Because *I'm* going to be president."

"No, you won't," Cassidy said. "*I'll* be the class president."

While the kids argued, Huxley licked peanut butter from the buttons. "This is crazy," Jeff told his friends. "Everyone knows *I* would make the best president."

Cassidy shook her head. Her blond hair pulled loose from its ponytail. "I'd be the best class president ever."

"What's wrong with me?" Carla argued.

"Or me?" added Darla.

The kids in the class weren't the only ones arguing. Ozzy and Edgar hovered near the hallway door. They each thought they'd make the best classroom leader.

"I'll be president," Ozzy declared, "then everyone will HAVE to do what I say!"

"I should be president," Edgar said. "I'm a writer, so I would be good at writing laws that YOU would have to obey."

Ozzy was so mad, steam rolled out his ears.

Edgar stuck out his tongue. Ozzy grabbed Edgar's tongue and twirled him around the room like a lasso.

Nina and Huxley ducked in the corner to avoid being hit by Edgar's twirling boots. "Something has to be done," Nina told Huxley. "And FAST!"

7
Ants

One little jingle. One little jangle.

Ozzy let go of Edgar's tongue. Edgar soared across the room and into a map of the United States. His boots stuck out of Texas for just a second before they disappeared. In that same instant, Ozzy vanished.

Olivia, the school janitor, showed up at the door. "What's all the ruckus?" she asked.

Since Mr. Morton wasn't in the room yet, Jeff answered, "We're holding a class election."

Cassidy nodded. "Everyone wants to be president."

Olivia laughed and the keys hanging from her red overalls jingled and jangled. "You should be like these guys." She held up a glass box and the kids crowded around to see. Olivia always had some new pet to show.

"That's just a box of dirt," Andrew said.

Olivia shook her head and her earrings dangled. "Look closer."

The kids peered inside the box. Carla squealed. Darla shrieked, "They're ants!"

"Cool," Jeff said, staring at hundreds of tiny ants crawling through tunnels in the dirt.

"That's disgusting," Carla said, backing away.

Olivia chuckled. "Maybe you could learn something from these little creatures. Why, these tiny fellows can solve problems ten times bigger than they are because ants work together."

Olivia left, taking her ant farm with her.

"Olivia just gave me an idea," Nina told the kids. "We should work together, too."

Cassidy patted her friend on the back.

"Nina's right. We should stop arguing and think about what's best for the class."

Darla nodded. "I'm tired . . ."

". . . of fighting," Carla finished.

"You know," Jeff said. "I'd rather make movies. I don't even *want* to be president."

"Really?" Cassidy asked.

Jeff nodded. "I'll vote for you, instead."

"I'll vote for Cassidy, too," Nina said.

Carla nodded. "We will . . ."

". . . too," Darla finished.

Carla and Darla cheered together. "Cassidy for president!"

Alex jumped between the twins and stopped them mid-cheer. "I'm not voting for a girl," he said.

"Don't worry," Andrew told him. "*I'm* still going to be president. There's no way Cassidy could beat me."

Nina jumped in between Andrew and Cassidy. "I know exactly how we can settle this once and for all."

8
The Boss

"A debate!" Mr. Morton said when Nina told him her idea. "Perfect! But first, we have some studying to do."

"Studying?" Becky blurted. "That doesn't sound like fun." She kicked the wall, and her ghostly foot sunk in up to her knee.

Andrew groaned and rolled his eyes. He must have felt the same way, even though he couldn't see or hear Becky. He also didn't know that Ozzy was floating around his desk. Ozzy spun his head around and around until it turned orange and bumpy like a basketball. "Vote for me," Ozzy said, "and school will be a BALL!"

When Becky finally tugged her foot free from the wall, she did a somersault

beside Ozzy and yelled, “I don’t want to be president anymore. Debates and studying? That’s boring!” She flipped across the room and the breeze she created spilled Andrew’s four hundred brightly colored crayons onto the floor.

“Someone knocked over my crayons,” Andrew complained.

Carla and Darla helped Andrew pick up the mess. Cassidy giggled but got quiet when Mr. Morton began the lesson.

“There are three parts, or branches,

of the government of the United States: the executive, the legislative, and the judiciary."

Becky yawned and popped out of sight. Nina agreed with Becky. All those big words didn't sound very interesting, but Nina kept listening.

"Today, we're talking about the executive branch," Mr. Morton continued. He held up a poster that had the word **PRESIDENT** printed in big, black letters at the top.

"The President is the head of the executive branch," Mr. Morton said.

"Yeah!" Andrew said as he stuffed crayons back into his box. "He's the boss. The President can do whatever he wants!"

"Not exactly," Mr. Morton explained. "There's something called checks and balances."

"My mom writes checks all the time," Carla told the class.

Darla giggled. "But she says it never balances."

Mr. Morton shook his head. “Checks and balances in government are different. If the President does something against the law, he can be impeached.”

“They throw peaches at him?” Andrew asked.

Ozzy must have thought the same thing because he threw rotten ghost peaches at Andrew. Andrew shivered as the invisible squishy fruit flew through his body.

“No, they have a hearing. If he is found guilty, he’s not President anymore.” Mr. Morton took off his glasses and wiped them with a tissue.

“Andrew would never last long as a president,” Carla said.

“He’s always breaking the rules,” Darla added. “So everyone should vote for Cassidy.”

Before the kids could start arguing again, Mr. Morton grabbed a piece of chalk and wrote six letters across the board. Each letter was three feet tall.

DEBATE!

PRESIDENT

When he finished writing, Mr. Morton faced the kids. "Our president will not have to worry about being impeached as long as we are careful with our votes."

"What does our vote have to do with the class president getting in trouble?" Nina asked.

Mr. Morton looked at the kids. "Voting is a very important right of citizens," he said. "You don't want to vote for someone you think will get into trouble. We'll have the debate tomorrow afternoon to see what each candidate believes in. But first, our class will have a *primary* election. Ready or not, it's time to vote to decide the top two candidates."

9
A Debate Disaster

"I can't believe I won the primary," Cassidy told her two friends the next day. They had just finished eating lunch and were heading back to the classroom. The big debate was just minutes away, and Cassidy was worried about how to answer the questions.

"I can't believe Andrew is the other candidate," Jeff grumbled. "The people who voted for him are crazy."

"It's because he's promising them all sorts of things," Cassidy said. "I have to promise even better stuff so people will vote for me in the real election. Do you have any ideas, Nina?"

Nina had been following her friends, but she wasn't really listening. She had other things on her mind.

"Nina?" Cassidy poked her friend in the arm. "Did you hear me?"

Nina shook her head. "I'm sorry. I was worrying about the election."

"That's exactly what I was talking about," Cassidy said, her hands on her hips. "What should I do?"

"It's not you I'm worried about," Nina said. "It's Ozzy and Edgar." Then she told her friends what she had seen the day before.

"While the rest of the class was

voting for the top two candidates," Nina explained, "I noticed the ghosts holding a primary election of their own. But their election was a little scary. Instead of writing names on paper, Ozzy and Edgar wrestled in the back of the room. They were fighting, and they were serious. What will happen when neither of them wins the election?"

In the classroom, Mr. Morton cleared his throat and looked down at the stack of index cards in his hands. Earlier in the day, kids had written questions on the cards.

Cassidy and Jeff didn't answer. They couldn't. They were both scared speechless at the thought of what two angry ghosts might do to their classroom.

"Andrew will begin the debate," Mr. Morton explained. "The first question is, How would you make our classroom a better place?"

Andrew grinned. "Once I'm president, we won't have to do another lick of homework ever again. I'd also make them serve pizza every day in the cafeteria. And, we'd have two hours of recess after lunch!"

A group of boys let out a whooping cheer. Even Jeff was smiling. Carla and

Darla were the only ones in the class who gasped.

"Ghosts NEVER do homework," Ozzy said, flying above Andrew.

It was Cassidy's turn to answer, so she waved Ozzy out of the way. "No homework is a good rule," she said, "but sometimes we have to do homework so we can learn. That's why I would make it a rule that homework could only be fun things. And if kids already knew how to do the work, then I'd let them have recess all day long. Better yet, they wouldn't even have to come to school. Unless," Cassidy added with a glare at Andrew, "you were a boy that misbehaved. Then you would have to do REAL work while the rest of us had fun."

"That's a stupid answer," Andrew snapped.

"Is not," Cassidy said.

"Is too!" Ozzy hollered.

"IS!" Alex and Andrew yelled.

"ISN'T!" Barbara yelled back.

Mr. Morton clapped his hands for order. When he did, he dropped the debate cards. He was too busy gathering them up to stop the class from arguing.

Edgar clasped his hands in front of his chest. “No, no, no,” he muttered as he floated between the desks to the front of the room. “The question wasn’t about homework,” Edgar told everyone, but Nina was the only one that heard him.

“It was about making things better for our class,” Edgar said, “and for all of Sleepy Hollow. We should be talking about how to make kids learn more. We ought to discuss how kids can help our town.”

"You're right," Nina said quietly as all around her the other kids shouted back and forth. Ghosts puffed up like balloons. Mr. Morton crawled on the floor, picking up note cards. No one but Nina knew that Edgar was trying to answer the question.

Nina shook her head. If all this happened after just one question during a debate, what would happen during the election? The whole thing was a debate disaster.

10
Impossible

"You should've listened to Edgar," Nina suggested to Cassidy that afternoon.

The rest of the third graders had filed out the door to go home. Nina, Cassidy, and Jeff were the last ones left in the room. The last ones, that is, besides the ghosts. The ghosts were always there. They *lived* in the basement of Sleepy Hollow Elementary, and right now Ozzy and Edgar hovered over the three friends.

"Why should I listen to a ghost?" Cassidy asked.

"Edgar had some very good ideas," Nina explained.

"I had good ideas, too," Ozzy bragged as he rolled up to Nina like a giant wagon

wheel. He stopped just inches from her nose. "Admit it."

Nina backed away from Ozzy. The last thing she wanted to do was make a bully ghost mad, and she didn't want to make her best friend angry, either. But she had no choice. She had to tell them the truth. "Your ideas were like Andrew's and Cassidy's," Nina said. "There's no way those ideas would work. Teachers would be mad. The principal would be mad. Even our parents would be mad. In the end, you would all make terrible class presidents because none of your ideas would work. You would know that if you had bothered to listen to Edgar."

Cassidy and Ozzy were quiet as they thought about what Nina said. Finally, Cassidy looked at Edgar. "I'm sorry I didn't listen to you," she said. "What were you trying to tell us?"

Edgar turned pink, then red, and finally purple. He ended up looking like a big grape. "Well . . . er . . . um . . ."

"Don't tell me you forgot," Ozzy said.

Edgar held up his journal. "I wrote it down," he said. "I write down everything." He opened his journal and read. When he was finished, the kids still looked at him. "Please stop staring," he said.

"A president has to get used to being the center of attention," Cassidy pointed out.

The color drained from Edgar until he was barely visible.

Nina felt sorry for Edgar. He had good ideas, and he actually might have made a good class president, but he was way too shy.

"There has to be a way to make this work," Nina said.

Edgar shook his head. "There is no way to please everyone," he said. "It's impossible."

Nina looked at Edgar and Ozzy. She looked at Cassidy and Jeff. "I don't believe in that word," Nina said. "*Nothing* is impossible. NOTHING!"

11
And the Winner Is . . .

The day of the class election finally arrived. Kids were already on the playground when Nina, Cassidy, and Jeff got there. Nina wore a red, white, and blue shirt in honor of President's Day.

"We have to vote for Andrew," Randy was shouting. "Boys rule!"

The rest of the boys chanted, "Boys rule! Boys rule! Boys rule!"

Cassidy sighed. "You know what?" she asked her two best friends. "I don't even want to be class president anymore. It's just too much trouble."

Carla and Darla yelled back at the chanting boys, "Girls are best! Girls are best!"

Allison and Barbara shoved two of the boys. The boys shoved them back.

Nina wedged herself between them so they had to stop shoving.

"When Andrew wins, he's going to turn our classroom into a mud pit," Randy bragged. "So you girls better get used to making mud pies."

"Do you really think the principal would allow a mud pit at school?" Nina asked.

"Not really," somebody muttered.

"That's why Cassidy needs to be president," Allison said. "Then we wouldn't even have to come to school as long as we knew stuff."

"Do you really think your parents would let you stay home?" Nina asked.

Everyone grew quiet as they thought about what Nina had said. While they were thinking, Nina began to speak. Her voice was soft and low so the rest of the kids had to lean forward to hear.

"Voting for a class leader isn't about

being a girl or a boy," Nina reminded them. "It's not about being the most popular, either. We should forget all that and think about the person that makes good decisions. Someone who has everyone's best interests in mind. The person that will listen to everybody's side and then work hard to make the fairest choices. So instead of fighting, you should be thinking. Thinking about the best and the fairest person to lead our classroom."

The kids did think. They were still thinking when the principal opened the doors and allowed the kids to file inside. When Mr. Morton handed out the election ballots so the kids could vote, they were still lost in thought.

"Remember," Mr. Morton said, "to vote for the person who would make the best decisions for everyone."

The ghosts fluttered over Mr. Morton as he collected the ballots and tallied the results. For once, the classroom was quiet. The kids. The ghosts. Everyone.

When Mr. Morton finished counting, he rubbed chalk dust from his glasses and squinted at the numbers on his paper. He took off his glasses and rubbed them even more with the tail of his shirt. Then he put them back on and leaned close to make sure he was reading everything right. Finally, he looked up and cleared his throat.

"Very strange results," he told the class. "Very strange indeed."

Carla couldn't stand the suspense. "Tell us . . ."

". . . the winner," Darla finished.

"It seems," Mr. Morton said, "that the winner is NINA!"

"Nina!" Andrew gasped.

"Nina?" Cassidy asked.

"NINA! NINA! NINA!" all the ghosts chanted at the same time.

Mr. Morton smiled. "More people voted for Nina as a write-in candidate than for Cassidy or Andrew. She's the official winner."

"But I was supposed to win," Andrew said. "Why did you vote for Nina?"

"She thinks of everyone," somebody from the back of the room blurted.

"She told the truth," Barbara said.

Then the entire class cheered for Nina. Even the ghosts.

"Congratulations," Mr. Morton said when the cheering finally died down. "Your picture will be the last one on our timeline."

Nina stood up tall. “Not just my picture,” she said. “But EVERYONE’S picture.”

“What do you mean?” Mr. Morton said.

“A president doesn’t do the job all alone,” she explained. “I’ll need everyone’s help, so everybody’s picture should be on the timeline.”

The class cheered even louder than before.

“We’ll need a representative for the boys and one for the girls,” Nina went on

when they were ready to listen. Then she looked at the ghosts floating over the heads of her classmates. "And, well, maybe a few more representatives as well. Together, we'll make decisions that work for the whole class."

"Vote for me! Vote for me!" kids yelled. "I want to be a representative!"

Jeff rolled his eyes. "Oh, no," he said. "Here we go again!"

Cassidy slapped Nina on the back, "Nina is truly red, white, and blue for her class."

"She's more than that," Ozzy said, floating above the kids. "She's red, white, and BOO!"

About the Authors

Marcia Thornton Jones and Debbie Dadey got into the *spirit* of writing when they worked together at the same school in Lexington, Kentucky. Since then, Debbie has *haunted* several states. She currently *haunts* Ft. Collins, CO, with her three children, three dogs, and husband. Marcia remains in Lexington, KY, where she lives with her husband and two cats.

Debbie and Marcia have fun with spooky stories. They have scared themselves silly with *The Adventures of the Bailey School Kids* and *The Bailey School Kids Jr. Chapter Books* series. Debbie also writes the *Swamp Monster in Third Grade* series, as well as some single titles like her upcoming book, *The Worst Name in the Third Grade*. Marcia's middle-grade novel, *Champ*, is due out later this year. To find out more about Debbie and Marcia, be sure to visit their Web site at: www.BaileyKids.com.

Red, White, and BOO Challenges!

- Becky thinks that Grover Cleveland is still president. Did you know that Grover Cleveland was the only president elected twice, but not twice in a row? He never went to college and was famous for his motto, "Tell the truth." Can you find out other interesting facts about Grover Cleveland? List them here!

  ____

  ____

  ____

  ____

- Do you know who is really president of the United States today?

  ____

- Find out the answer to Nina's question — were there cars one hundred years ago? ____________________

- What about computers? (A hint: When Debbie and Marcia were young, no one had computers in their house. The only computers were larger than most rooms.) ____________________

- Did they have TVs one hundred years ago? ____________________
  Movies? ____________________

- Can you find a book in the library about what things were like one hundred years ago? ____________________

- Debbie recently took a trip to Mount Rushmore. Do you know which presidents have their likenessess carved there?

  ____

  ____

  ____

  ____

- On a separate sheet of paper, create your own timeline of the presidents!

- Did you know?
  In 1875, the submarine was invented.
  In 1885, the motorcycle was invented.
  In 1896, the radio was invented.
  In 1899, aspirin was introduced.

Ready for more spooky fun?
Then take a sneak peek at the next

Ghostville Elementary®

#17 No Haunting Zone

No more homework.
No more books.
No more . . . SCHOOL!

The town board wants to tear down Sleepy Hollow Elementary and build a brand-new school. Cool, right? Not quite! If the old school is gone, what will happen to the ghost class living in the basement?

Will they disappear forever . . . or will they be free to haunt the entire town? Nina and her friends have to do something — and QUICK! Or it's bye-bye, BOO-tiful basement. Hello, haunted hollow!